Series 522

The story of
Joseph

by LUCY DIAMOND

with illustrations by
KENNETH INNS

Ladybird Books Loughborough

THE STORY OF JOSEPH

Long ago, in the land of Canaan, a rich shepherd prince lived in Hebron by the oaks of Mamre.

His name was Jacob—but afterwards God named him Israel—" a soldier of God."

Jacob had twelve sons. He loved them dearly, but best of all he loved the two youngest—Joseph and Benjamin. They were the sons of his dear wife Rachel, who had died. The brothers were all shepherds and worked together in the fields.

Sad to say, Joseph sometimes told tales to his father of what his brothers did. This made them very angry!

When Joseph was seventeen, Jacob gave him " a coat of many colours "—a long sleeved garment, only worn by those who had no work to do.

When the brothers saw Joseph wearing this grand new coat, they were furious!

One night Joseph dreamed, and he told the dream to his brothers.

" Listen," he said, " we were binding sheaves in the fields, and my sheaf stood upright. Then all your sheaves came round and bowed down to my sheaf ! "

How cross the brothers were !

Once more Joseph had a dream and he hastened to tell his brothers :

" I have dreamed another dream! I saw the sun and the moon and eleven stars, and they all bowed down to me ! "

Even Jacob was angry with Joseph this time, and scolded him:

" Do you think that I and your brothers will ever come to bow ourselves down to you ? "

This made his brothers hate Joseph more than ever, but his father kept these strange dreams in mind.

What could they mean ?

Some time after this the brothers had gone far north to Shechem to feed their flocks. Israel said to Joseph:

" Go to Shechem and see how your brothers are getting on. Bring me word how they are."

So Joseph left the Vale of Hebron and journeyed to Shechem. His brothers were not there! He was wandering about looking for them, when he met a man, and spoke to him:

" I want to find my brothers. Have you seen them about here?"

" Yes," the man answered, " I saw them with their flocks. They said they were going to Dothan to find fresh pasture."

So Joseph went on till he came to Dothan, which was quite near the great highway on which caravans travelled from Damascus to the Land of Egypt.

When the brothers in Dothan saw Joseph coming towards them quite alone, all the bitter hatred they had hidden in their hearts for so long flared up.

" Look ! " they said, " here is that dreamer coming. Let us kill him and throw him into one of the pits. We can say an evil beast has eaten him. We shall see then what will become of his dreams ! "

The eldest brother, Reuben, who was just going off to water his sheep, tried to save him. " Don't kill him," he said. " Cast him into a pit if you will, but lay no hand upon him."

Reuben really meant to keep Joseph alive, and take him safely home!

So as Joseph drew near, the brothers seized him, tore off the beautiful coat his father had given him, and threw him into a dry, empty pit nearby.

And while Joseph lay helpless in the pit, the brothers sat down to eat the food he had brought.

As they ate and talked together they saw a long train of camels coming along the great road which led by Dothan. A band of Ishmaelites were going down into the Land of Egypt carrying spices and rich merchandise.

This gave Judah, another brother, an idea.

" What good will it do us to kill our brother?" he said, " let us sell him to these Ishmaelites, then we shall be rid of him."

So Joseph was hurriedly drawn from the pit, and sold to the Ishmaelites for twenty pieces of silver.

When Reuben came back from tending his flock, he was terribly distressed to find Joseph gone. All he could do now was to help make up a story to tell their father.

The brothers killed a goat, and taking Joseph's coat, they dipped it in its blood. Then they carried it home to their father in Hebron.

" Look ! " they cried, " we have found this by the way. Is it Joseph's coat?"

Israel took one look! He knew that coat —the grand coat he had given to his beloved son!

" It is my son's coat," he cried. " An evil beast must have devoured him. Joseph must be dead ! "

And Israel wept with such bitter sorrow that the brothers almost wished the thing undone—but they dared not speak the truth. They tried to comfort their father, but Israel's grief was terrible.

" I will go down to the grave mourning for my son," he cried.

And no one could bring him comfort.

. . . . .

The Ishmaelites carried Joseph with them into the Land of Egypt. They were pleased they had bought this strong, handsome lad. He would fetch a good price in the market.

There Joseph was sold as a slave.

The man who bought him was Potiphar, the captain of the king's guard.

How sad it was for Joseph then—far from his home—quite alone in a strange land! This favourite son of a loving father now had to face loneliness and many hardships during the years which followed. But he was no coward! He was brave and patient, and in his loneliness his thoughts turned to the Lord Jehovah. Even in this strange land he felt that God was very near.

" And the Lord was with Joseph, and made all that he did to prosper."

Potiphar took Joseph home and treated his young slave kindly. He soon found that Joseph could be trusted, and made him steward of his household, and of all that he had.

" And the Lord blessed Potiphar for Joseph's sake."

Then the lies of a wicked woman turned the captain against his slave. Angrily he flung him into prison ! What a terrible thing !

But Joseph was still brave and patient, and the keeper of the prison liked and trusted him, and let him take charge of the other prisoners.

Among these were the king's butler and baker. One morning Joseph found them looking very worried.

" What is the matter ? " he asked.

" We have dreamed," they answered, " and we do not know what the dreams mean."

" Tell me your dreams," Joseph said. " God will show me the meaning."

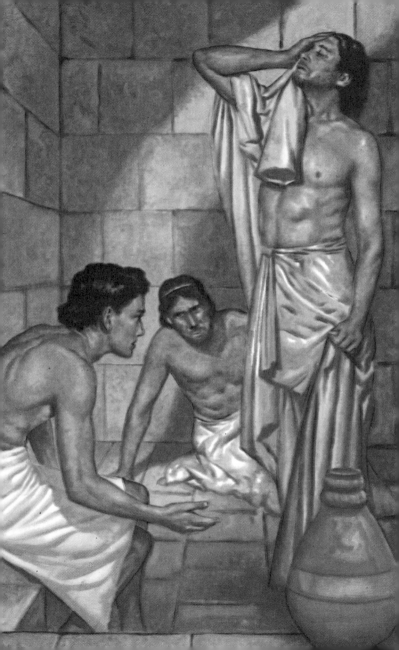

So the chief butler told his dream: " I saw a vine with three branches. The vine budded and blossomed into clusters of grapes. Pharaoh's cup was in my hand, and I pressed the grapes into the cup and gave it to Pharaoh."

" The three branches are three days," Joseph answered. " In three days Pharaoh will make you his butler again."

The chief baker hastened to tell his dream. Alas! the meaning was a sad one:

" Pharaoh will never forgive you," Joseph told him.

Then he turned to the butler:

"When you stand again before Pharaoh," he pleaded, " do tell him about me. I was stolen away from the land of the Hebrews and here I have done no wrong—yet I am in prison."

Everything happened as Joseph had foretold—but the chief butler forgot all about Joseph!

Two years passed, and Joseph was still in prison.

One night Pharaoh dreamed that he was standing by the river Nile, when seven fat kine came from the river and fed on the reed grass.

Then there came seven miserably thin kine—and they ate up the seven fat kine.

Pharaoh awoke—but again he slept, and dreamed another dream.

He saw seven ears of corn spring up on one stalk, all good and full. After them came seven thin ears, dried and scorched by the wind! And the thin ears swallowed up the seven full ears!

When Pharaoh awoke he was troubled. None of his wise men could tell what the dreams meant and so he grew more anxious.

Then the butler at last remembered Joseph and told the king about him.

" Send for this man," Pharaoh ordered.

Joseph was hurriedly fetched from prison to stand before the king.

" I have dreamed a dream," Pharaoh said. " I hear that you can interpret dreams."

" I cannot tell their meanings," Joseph replied, " but God will give Pharaoh an answer."

So to this Hebrew slave Pharaoh told his dream.

" The dream is a good one," Joseph explained. " The seven fat kine and the seven good ears of corn are seven years. The seven lean kine and the seven poor ears are seven years. There shall be seven years of plenty in Egypt—then will come seven years of famine—such a grievous famine that the years of plenty will be forgotten! Famine will be everywhere, and will eat up the land.

That is the meaning of the dreams, O king. God will bring all this to pass."

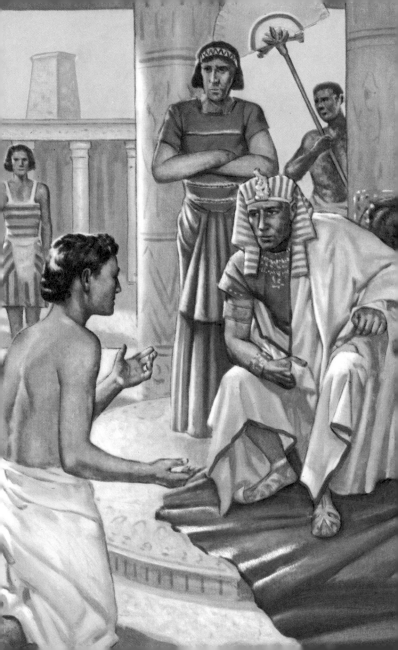

There was a hushed silence as Joseph finished speaking. Pharaoh looked thoughtfully on this Hebrew slave who stood so quietly and fearlessly before him. He felt certain that what he had foretold would come true.

" What can we do ? " he asked.

Joseph answered at once.

" Let Pharaoh look out a man wise and sensible, and set him over the Land of Egypt. Let him gather corn and store it safely away during the seven years of plenty. Then when famine comes there will be food in the land, and the people will not die."

Pharaoh listened carefully. He looked around. There were all his courtiers, with the wise men and magicians! They had not been able to help him! Could he choose any of them ?

Then he looked again at Joseph!

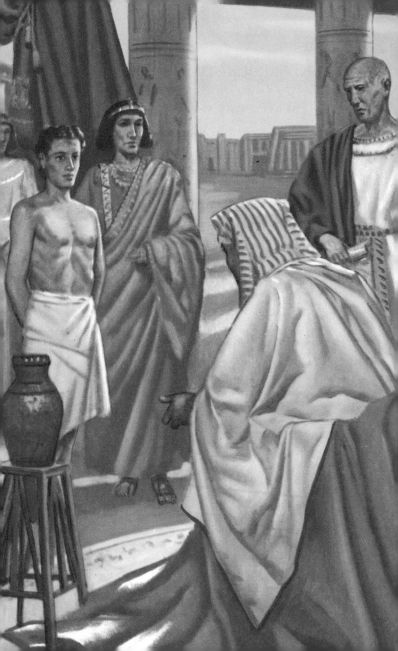

At last Pharaoh spoke:

" Where can we find such a wise and sensible man as this Hebrew—a man in whom the Spirit of God is ! "

" God has shown you His will," he said to Joseph. " Among all my people there is none so discreet and wise as you. You will be able to help and advise us. You shall be over my people and over my house. You shall be ruler second only to me in all the land."

Pharaoh took off his ring and placed it on Joseph's hand. He dressed him in fine robes, and put a gold chain around his neck.

Now Joseph was Governor of all Egypt, and when he rode out in his chariot, runners went before him crying: " Bow the knee ! Bow the knee! "

Joseph was thirty years old when he became a ruler in Egypt. Now he had a great work to do.

During the seven years of plenty he never rested. He went up and down the land, seeing that corn was safely harvested. He built huge storehouses, and stored away all the food the people did not need. When these were filled he built others, until at last when famine came there was food in Egypt.

Joseph opened his great storehouses and as the famine grew worse, starving people came to him for food.

Famine spread. In the Land of Canaan it was grievous.

One day Israel said to his sons: " I hear there is corn in Egypt. Go down and buy for us that we may live and not die."

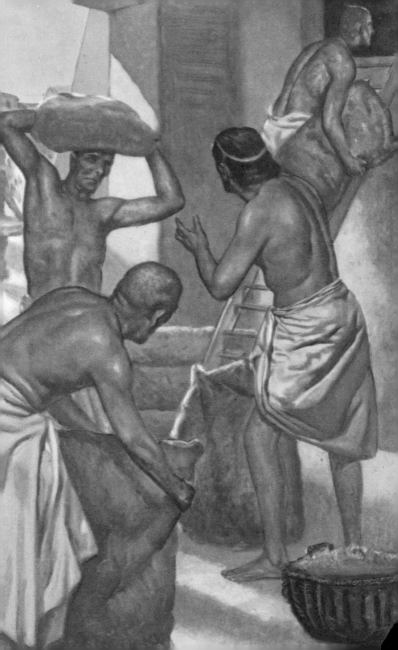

So Joseph's brothers went down into Egypt to buy corn. Benjamin alone stayed behind with his father.

And Joseph was the Governor to whom they came to buy, and they bowed themselves low before him!

The dreamer whose dreams had come true, marvelled at the strange ways by which God had brought him to this moment! He knew his brothers, but they did not know him. How could they ever think that this majestic Governor of Egypt was the brother they had sold into slavery!

There was no hardness nor unforgiveness in the heart of the man who had become so wise a ruler, but Joseph felt he must know if they were sorry for what they had done, and how they had treated his father and Benjamin.

Joseph began by speaking roughly to his brothers:

" Who are you, and where do you come from ? " he asked.

" We are ten brothers," they answered. " We come from the Land of Canaan."

Joseph pretended not to believe them.

" You are spies, and no true men," he said. " Are all your father's sons here ? "

" No," they replied. " Our youngest brother is with our father—and one is dead."

Joseph still pretended to doubt them. He had them put in prison for three days. Then he said:

" I will not kill you, for I fear God, but I will see if you speak the truth. One of you shall stay in prison while the others go back and bring your youngest brother here."

The brothers were in great trouble! They talked among themselves, never dreaming that this stern Governor could understand.

"We are to blame for our brother's death," they said, "and this truly is our punishment. We took no notice of his distress, and now this has come upon us."

Joseph heard—and he went out and wept. But he was still firm. He had Simeon bound and put into prison, and told the others to go home. He ordered his servants to fill their sacks with corn, and to put the money they had brought into each sack. Then he gave them food for their journey.

How amazed the brothers were when they opened their sacks and found the money. They were afraid! They were still more worried when they had to tell their father what had happened!

Israel was broken-hearted.

"Benjamin shall not go with you," he said. "His brother is dead, and only he is left me."

The famine grew worse.

" We dare not go back to Egypt without Benjamin," the brothers said.

It was only after Reuben and Judah had promised to guard their youngest brother with their lives that Israel gave way—but he mourned grievously.

They set out laden with presents for the Governor, and taking back the money found in their sacks.

When Joseph saw Benjamin, he went out and wept for joy. He longed to make himself known—but wished still to test his brothers.

He invited Simeon and all of them to a feast in his house. He sent them meat from his own table, but he sent Benjamin five times as much as the others, and the brothers showed no signs of envy. They were all happy together!

That night Joseph ordered his steward to fill his visitors' sacks with corn, and to put every man's money inside his sack.

" Put my silver cup with his money inside the youngest brother's sack," he told them.

The steward did as his master ordered, and the next morning the brothers started for home.

Then Joseph called his steward and said:

" Hurry, go after those men and say: Why have you given evil for good? Why have you stolen my Lord's silver cup? "

" God forbid that we should do such a thing " the brothers said, when the steward overtook them.

" Search our sacks, and if it be found with any of us he must die."

How horrified the brothers were when the cup was found in Benjamin's sack! The steward would only have taken Benjamin, but all the brothers turned back with him.

They came back to Joseph's house, and bowed themselves to the ground before him.

"What is this you have done?" the Governor asked them sternly.

"The man in whose sack my cup was found shall be my slave. As for you others —go back in peace!"

Then Judah came near, and spoke:

"O my Lord, I am your servant! Do not be angry, but let me say one word. We have a father, an old man—and my youngest brother is very precious to him. His brother is dead, and my father loves him above us all."

Judah went on to tell the sorrowful story of Israel's great loss and of his grief.

"Let me be your slave instead of the lad," he begged. "I cannot go back to my father without him."

At this Joseph could hold back no longer. He saw how changed his brothers were, and he knew that he, too, had learned many lessons through the lonely years. Now he loved his brothers, and longed after his own people. He sent all his servants out, and the Governor stood alone as he made himself known to his brothers.

" I am Joseph! Tell me about my father."

The brothers were terrified! How could this great Lord be the lad they had called " the dreamer", and sold as a slave into Egypt! Surely he would kill them now he had them in his power! But Joseph understood.

" Come near to me," he said. " You must not grieve and be angry with yourselves because you sold me. God sent me here before you because He had work planned for me, and to save many lives."

" Now," Joseph went on, " hurry back to my father and tell him that I am alive, and long to see him. The famine is still bad, so my father must come here quickly with all of you and your children. There is plenty of food for you all. The Egyptians are not shepherds, so you shall have the Land of Goshen for yourselves, where there is good pasture for your flocks."

Then Joseph kissed his brothers, and tenderly drew Benjamin close to him.

Pharaoh was pleased when he heard the news. He told Joseph to send wagons for his father and the children to bring them to Egypt.

Joseph gave them presents and sent ten asses laden with good things for his father.

" Don't quarrel by the way," he laughed as they set off.

So Israel saw his beloved son again after many years. At first he hardly dared to believe, but when he saw the wagons, and all the things sent for his comfort, he knew this marvellous news was true.

" It is enough," he cried. " Joseph my son is yet alive. I will go and see him before I die!"

We may think what a joyful day it was when Joseph rode out in his chariot to meet the caravan from Canaan. He ran to fling his arms around his father, and they both wept for joy. Through such sad and lonely years God had brought them to this happy meeting!

Joseph took his father to see Pharaoh, who was very gracious to him. Then Israel thanked the king and blessed him.

Israel and all his family settled in the Land of Goshen, and the Egyptians called these strangers " the children of Israel " or Israelites.

Israel lived there for seventeen years, and rejoiced to see his son so wisely ruling the land. When he was dying he asked Joseph not to bury him in Egypt, but in Canaan, the land God had promised to his fathers.

Joseph and his brothers lived happily and peacefully together! For many years Joseph ruled the Land of Egypt, greatly loved by Pharaoh, and honoured and trusted by all the people.